# Dad, the Bird Caller

By Diana Noonan

Illustrations by Beth Norling

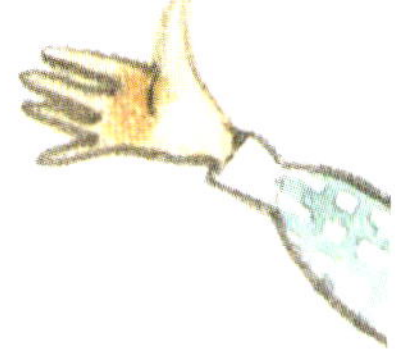

## Contents

Chapter 1

# A Play about Birds

At school, we were getting ready to put on a play about birds.

"Who can bring feathers to make a bird hat?" asked our teacher, Ms Lim.

“I can,” I said.

“Thank you, Milly,” said Ms Lim.

“I can bring a box to make a bird beak,” said my twin brother, Ben.

“Great!” said Ms Lim.

That night, we told Dad about the bird play.

"I like birds," said Dad.
"I can't wait to see the play.
When I was a boy, I could make a sound
like every bird in the bush."

Chapter 2

# Dad and the Bird Calls

The next day was Friday.
Dad came to school in the car to take us home.

But he didn't call out, "Hello!"
He stood by the car and went,
"*Warble … Warble*!"
*Everyone* could hear him!

All Saturday and Sunday,
Dad made loud bird calls.
He made them in his bedroom.
He made them in the park.

He even made bird calls at the market.
"Dad!" we said. "People are looking at us!"

"But I have to practise," said Dad.
"I want to be as good
as I was when I was a boy!"

The next week at school,
I helped paint a tree for the play.
Ben found bird calls
on the school computer.

Ms Lim said Ben could be our sound man.

On the day of the play, we had one last practice.
It was on the stage in the school hall.

Ben sat at the side of the stage
beside the computer.

Ms Lim sat near him.
When it was time for the bird calls,
Ben played them on the computer.

Chapter 3

# The Night of the Play

That night, everyone came to see the play.
Dad sat right at the front of the stage.
He gave me a little smile.

As the play was about to begin,
Ms Lim said quietly,
"Give us the first bird call, Ben."

But the computer wouldn't work!
"It's no good, Ms Lim," said Ben.
"The computer won't go!"

"Dad could help," I said.
"He can make bird calls."

Ms Lim looked down at Dad.
"Would you help us, please, Mr Jordan?"
she said.

Dad was so happy!
He stood beside the computer.
He made bird calls when Ben told him to.

We were so proud of Dad.

At the end of the play,
everyone gave a big cheer for Dad.
My brother and I gave him a big hug.
"You can make your bird calls anywhere!"
we said.

Dad gave us a smile.
“Even at the market?” he laughed.